BALLPARK
Mysteries 17
THE
TRIPLE
PLAY
TWINS

Also by David A. Kelly
BALLPARK MYSTERIES®

#1 *The Fenway Foul-Up*

#2 *The Pinstripe Ghost*

#3 *The L.A. Dodger*

#4 *The Astro Outlaw*

#5 *The All-Star Joker*

#6 *The Wrigley Riddle*

#7 *The San Francisco Splash*

#8 *The Missing Marlin*

#9 *The Philly Fake*

#10 *The Rookie Blue Jay*

#11 *The Tiger Troubles*

#12 *The Rangers Rustlers*

#13 *The Capital Catch*

#14 *The Cardinals Caper*

#15 *The Baltimore Bandit*

#16 *The Colorado Curveball*

#17 *The Triple Play Twins*

SUPER SPECIAL #1 *The World Series Curse*

SUPER SPECIAL #2 *Christmas in Cooperstown*

SUPER SPECIAL #3 *Subway Series Surprise*

SUPER SPECIAL #4 *The World Series Kids*

THE MVP SERIES

#1 *The Gold Medal Mess*

#2 *The Soccer Surprise*

#3 *The Football Fumble*

#4 *The Basketball Blowout*

Babe Ruth and the Baseball Curse

BALLPARK Mysteries 17

THE TRIPLE PLAY TWINS

by David A. Kelly

illustrated by Mark Meyers

A STEPPING STONE BOOK™

Random House 🏠 New York

This book is dedicated to kids who don't like to read or have a hard time reading. I know I did. Stick with it. Remember, reading is like downloading games. You can reprogram your brain just by reading a book!
—D.A.K.

"My father used to play with my brother and me in the yard. Mother would come out and say, 'You're tearing up the grass.' 'We're not raising grass,' Dad would reply. 'We're raising boys.'"
—Harmon Killebrew, the Minnesota Twins' greatest hitter, thirteen-time All-Star, and member of the National Baseball Hall of Fame

Text copyright © 2021 by David A. Kelly

Cover art and interior illustrations copyright © 2021 by Mark Meyers

All rights reserved. Published in the United States by Random House Children's Books, a division of Penguin Random House LLC, New York.

Random House and the colophon are registered trademarks and A Stepping Stone Book and the colophon are trademarks of Penguin Random House LLC. Ballpark Mysteries® is a registered trademark of Upside Research, Inc.

Visit us on the Web!
rhcbooks.com

Educators and librarians, for a variety of teaching tools, visit us at
RHTeachersLibrarians.com

Library of Congress Cataloging-in-Publication Data
Names: Kelly, David A. (David Andrew), author. | Meyers, Mark, illustrator.
Title: The triple play twins / by David A. Kelly; illustrated by Mark Meyers.
Description: New York: Random House, [2021] | Series: Ballpark mysteries; 17 | "A Stepping stone book." | Summary: "Cousins Mike and Kate investigate after Marco and Pedro, the twin players from the Minnesota Twins, are subjected to a water-balloon attack." —Provided by publisher
Identifiers: LCCN 2020028607 | ISBN 978-0-593-12624-0 (trade) | ISBN 978-0-593-12625-7 (lib. bdg.) | ISBN 978-0-593-12626-4 (ebook)
Subjects: CYAC: Baseball—Fiction. | Minnesota Twins (Baseball team)—Fiction. | Brothers—Fiction. | Twins—Fiction. | Cousins—Fiction. | Minnesota—Fiction. | Mystery and detective stories.
Classification: LCC PZ7.K2936 Tri 2021 | DDC [Fic]—dc23

Printed in the United States of America
10 9 8 7 6 5 4 3 2 1

This book has been officially leveled by using the F&P Text Level Gradient™ Leveling System.

Random House Children's Books supports the First Amendment
and celebrates the right to read.

Contents

Chapter 1   **A Splash Hit**   1

Chapter 2   **Sibling Rivalry**   9

Chapter 3   **Do Not Disturb**   20

Chapter 4   **Who's Lying?**   31

Chapter 5   **A Second Spotting**   40

Chapter 6   **A Third Possibility**   49

Chapter 7   **A Second Surprise!**   61

Chapter 8   **Out of Storage**   68

Chapter 9   **A Triple Play**   81

Chapter 10   **Triple Play Triplets**   91

**Dugout Notes ☆
Minnesota Twins**   99

A Splash Hit

"Hey, what's a pig doing at a baseball game?" Mike Walsh asked his cousin Kate Hopkins.

It was a warm summer night, and Mike and Kate were at a minor-league game in St. Paul, Minnesota, with Kate's mom. It was the bottom of the fifth inning, and a pig wearing a purple baseball cap and frilly purple outfit had just trotted out to the umpire near home plate.

"He's the St. Paul Saints' mascot," Kate said. "He's trained to bring out new baseballs!"

"I just hope he doesn't *hog* the ball!" Mike said as he nudged Kate.

The umpire opened a small box that was strapped to the pig's back and pulled out a fresh white baseball. But before the pig could return to its pen, the catcher caught it. He picked the pig up. Its feet dangled in the air. The catcher pointed the pig's pink snout at the umpire and nodded. The crowd yelled, "Kiss! Kiss! Kiss!"

The umpire waved his hands and turned his head away. But the crowd roared more and clapped louder. Finally, the umpire turned back. He held up his hands and leaned over. The catcher moved the pig forward.

The umpire gave the pig a big kiss!

"Yuck!" Mike said. He wiped his mouth on his arm.

The catcher put the pig down. It took off for its pen under the stands.

"Hey, I betcha don't know what position that pig plays," Mike said.

"No, what?" Kate asked.

"Short-*slop*!" Mike said as he collapsed into laughter.

The game resumed a moment later with the fresh, pig-delivered baseball. The St. Paul Saints' batter wasted no time in sending it out of the park. With a loud *WAP!* his bat connected with the first pitch for a home run! The fans cheered as he circled the bases. The Saints were now ahead of the Chicago Dogs by three runs!

Kate's mom, Mrs. Hopkins, leaned forward in her seat next to Kate. "I hope the *other* home team does just as well when we see *them* tomorrow night,"

she said. Mrs. Hopkins was a sports reporter. She often brought Mike and Kate with her when she traveled for work. "The cities of St. Paul and Minneapolis are so close together, they think of themselves as twins. People can root for the minor-league team in St. Paul and the major-league team in Minneapolis!"

"I guess that's why they call the Minneapolis team the Minnesota Twins," Mike said.

Mrs. Hopkins nodded. "Exactly. They were originally going to be called the Twin Cities Twins when they moved from Washington, D.C., in 1960," she said. "But they were named the Minnesota Twins instead."

"I read about that on the plane," Kate said. She loved to read. "That's why their big bear mascot is called T.C. Bear. It's short for Twin Cities Bear!"

Down on the field, the next St. Paul Saints

batter grounded out to end the inning.

"Wait until you see the giant neon sign near the Twins' scoreboard," Mrs. Hopkins said. "It has an outline of the state with twin baseball players standing on opposite sides of the Mississippi River shaking hands. They represent the cities of St. Paul and Minneapolis. Can you guess what their names are?"

"Fred and George?" Mike asked. "Like in Harry Potter?"

Mrs. Hopkins laughed and shook her head. "Good guess, but no. You need to be thinking about the names of the Twin Cities."

"How about Minnie and Paul?" Kate asked. "Like Minneapolis and St. Paul!"

"Yes, exactly!" Mrs. Hopkins said.

"Oh, I was just about to guess Marco and Pedro!" Mike said. "The twin Twins!"

The twin Twins were twin brothers who

played for the Minnesota Twins. Marco was their star second baseman, and Pedro was their star first baseman. They were famous for making triple plays, which are rare. Even though an average of only five triple plays are made each year among all major-league teams, Marco and Pedro had made three so far this season.

Mrs. Hopkins nodded. "That would have been a good guess, too," she said. "I'm going to interview them tomorrow for my article, but maybe I can introduce them to you after tonight's game."

Mike and Kate looked at each other and high-fived. "Cool!" Mike said. He pulled a black marker from his pocket and held it up with a baseball. "I'm going to ask them for their autographs! If they win two more games, the Twins will clinch a spot in the playoffs for the first time in a really long time!"

Neither team scored in the next inning, and soon the organ started blasting away for the seventh-inning stretch. Fans rose from their seats and sang "Take Me Out to the Ball Game." When the song ended, the announcer's voice boomed from the loudspeakers.

"And now, help me welcome the dynamic duo from our sister city. The one. The two. The only twin Twins!"

The crowd roared and clapped. Two tall baseball players in Minnesota Twins uniforms bounded out to the coach's box near first base. They took off their hats and waved as the crowd cheered. They had short buzz cuts and tall, muscular bodies. The twins picked up a large cardboard check for the children's hospital and held it in front of them. They waved and smiled.

Suddenly, there was a commotion above Mike's and Kate's seats.

"Heads up!" a fan called from behind them.

Everyone looked up. A large red object sailed through the air from the top of the stands.

It was headed right for the twin Twins!

They tried to escape, but it was too late to move.

A giant water balloon landed on their shoulders and exploded with a splash!

Sibling Rivalry

"Whoa!" Kate cried out. "That was a direct hit!"

"And not the kind you usually see in a baseball game," Mike said.

The twins were soaked. So was the giant cardboard check they were holding. A batboy ran over from the dugout with towels.

Kate turned and scanned the crowd. Most of the fans were watching the action on the field. But Kate saw a tall man with long blond hair jogging to the exit.

Kate nudged Mike. "Quick! There's a guy trying to get away. Let's follow him," she whispered. She turned to her mom. "We're going to check something out. We'll be back in a few minutes."

"Okay," her mom said.

Kate ran for the main level while Mike scrambled up the stairs behind her. At the top of the aisle, Kate made a beeline for the nearest

exit. Mike followed close behind. Just ahead was the man with blond hair.

He had stopped in front of the security guard at the exit. He turned around and glanced at the field. He was wearing a Chicago White Sox hat. He had small eyes that were close together and a bushy black mustache. Before Kate and Mike could reach him, he slipped past the guard and out of the ballpark.

Kate and Mike ran for the exit.

The security guard held up her hand. "Hold on, kids," she said. "Once you leave, you can't come back into the park."

Kate skidded to a stop. "It's important," she said. "Can we just go outside for a minute?"

The guard shook her head. "Sorry, I can't allow that."

Mike and Kate watched as the blond man jogged away from the park.

"Do you think he threw the balloon?" Mike asked.

Kate shrugged. "I didn't see him do it, but he was the only fan who wasn't looking at the field when I spotted him," she said. "Plus, why would he run away if he wasn't guilty? Something's not right."

"Maybe it was just a practical joke," Mike said. "Baseball players love to play practical jokes on each other. Especially famous ones like the twin Twins, I bet. I'm sure someone's jealous of them!"

"Maybe," Kate said. "Let's get back."

By the time Mike and Kate made it back to their seats, the twin Twins had left the field and the game had resumed. Two innings later, the St. Paul Saints pitcher struck out three batters and the game was over. The Saints had won!

Mrs. Hopkins stood up. "Let's go find the twin Twins," she said. "Hopefully they've dried off by now!"

The three made their way over to the Saints' dugout. Mrs. Hopkins talked to one of the security guards, and he let them onto the field. The twin Twins were standing near first base again and had just finished an interview with a TV crew. Mrs. Hopkins walked up and introduced herself, Mike, and Kate.

Marco and Pedro, the twin Twins, towered over Mike and Kate. They reached out to shake hands.

"I'm Marco," said the one on the left. "Nice to meet you!"

"And I'm Pedro," said the one on the right. "Nice to meet you!"

Mike and Kate shook their hands and looked from one twin to the other. They were identical.

"Wow! You guys really look the same," Mike said. "How can people tell you apart?"

Pedro and Marco straightened up. "We get that a lot," the one on the left said. "We really do look the same. Sometimes even *we* get confused."

The twin on the right nodded. "Yup," he said. He nudged his brother. "Actually, I think *I'm* Marco, and *you're* Pedro."

"Oh, maybe! Better check our numbers," the

twin on the left said. The twins turned around to show the numbers on their jerseys. They read 12 and 21.

"Yup!" the twin on the left said after Kate read the numbers off. "Pedro's number is twelve, and Marco's is twenty-one. So I guess I'm Pedro, not Marco. We're so identical it's hard to remember who's who!"

Pedro and Marco looked at each other for a moment and then broke up laughing! Mike, Kate, and Mrs. Hopkins joined in.

"We actually *do* remember our own names," Pedro said. "And you can tell us apart if you look at Marco's chin. He's got a little scar on it from when he was learning to ride a bike and fell off it!" Pedro smiled and pointed to his mouth. "And I've got a small chip on my front tooth from being hit by a ball!"

Mike and Kate studied the twins' faces.

"Yeah, you're right!" Mike said. "So I guess you're not *exactly* the same!"

"Nope," Pedro said. "Even though we look almost identical, there *are* some differences!"

"Like one of us is a better hitter!" Marco said, nudging his brother. "When's the last time you hit a home run? I hit at least one per week!"

Pedro smiled. "Check the statistics," he said. "Who's hit more doubles and runs batted in? That means *I'm* the better hitter!"

"Well, I think you're both great hitters," Mike said. He pulled a marker and a baseball from his pocket. "Would you be willing to sign my baseball?"

"Sure," the twins said in unison.

Pedro signed his name with the number 12, and Marco signed his with the number 21.

"Thanks!" Mike said. He studied the signatures. "Sweet! This one is going into our collection!" He slipped the ball into his pocket.

Kate pointed to a few wet spots on the sleeves of the twins' jerseys. "Looks like that water balloon soaked you two," she said. "Was that a practical joke by your teammates or something?"

Marco and Pedro looked at their damp uniforms and shook their heads.

"No, we have no idea who could have done
that," Marco said. "Maybe someone is trying to
throw us off our game so we don't get into the
playoffs!"

"Maybe," Pedro said. "But you know, if the
water balloon had just hit you, I would have
guessed it was Mom. She's always liked *me*
better than *you*."

Marco gave his brother a gentle shove. "She
does not," he said. "Plus, she couldn't tell us
apart anyway! I'll bet she thought *you* were
me!"

Pedro puffed out his chest and stared down
Marco for a moment. Then they both burst out
laughing again!

"But really, whoever it was had a pretty

good arm," Pedro said. "They threw it all the way from the main walkway!"

"We could use an arm like that for our game tomorrow night against the Milwaukee Brewers," Marco said. "We have to win the next two games to make the playoffs!"

Pedro nodded. "Hey, we should get going," he said. "Nice to meet you. Maybe we'll see you tomorrow night!"

"It's time for us to go, too," Mrs. Hopkins said. "We've got a big day tomorrow. A Minnesota Twins baseball game tomorrow night, and an afternoon at the biggest mall in America! You know, the one with the amusement park in it!"

"Oh, wow!" Mike said. He high-fived Kate. "Roller coasters, here we come!"

Do Not Disturb

"Watch out below!" Mike called out.

The giant floating log Kate and Mike were riding in bobbed along its water-filled track and zipped down an incline. It picked up speed until it splashed at the bottom and then started moving up an even larger hill.

"That was awesome!" Mike said. "Wait until the last drop. It's the biggest!"

Mike and Kate were at the amusement park in the center of the giant mall near the city of

Minneapolis. Kate's mom was shopping while Mike and Kate were exploring the rides. They had already gone on a Ferris wheel, a spinning flight machine, and a tall drop tower. After the log flume, they planned to hit the roller coaster that looped through the mall's center court area.

Mike and Kate's bobbing log floated past a huge replica of Paul Bunyan and Babe, his big ox. Kate nudged Mike and pointed at the giant lumberjack. "I read in a tall tales book that Minnesota's ten thousand lakes were created by Paul Bunyan's footsteps," she said.

"Well, I'm glad he's not stepping on us!" Mike said.

The log turned one last corner and teetered on the edge of a long drop. Below them, Mike and Kate could see shoppers and stores. Water swirled on both sides of the log as it started its plunge.

"Whee!" Kate yelled.

As the log flew down its watery flume, it splashed water on riders and shoppers. The log bobbed along until it reached a docking area, where an employee helped the riders get out.

"That was awesome!" Mike said. His shirt was soaked. "We have to do it again!"

Kate smiled and brushed some water drops off her face. "Let's do the roller coaster first."

"I've got a better idea," Mike said. "Let's see the baseball sights before the roller coaster."

Kate looked around. "We're in a mall! There are no baseball sights around here!" she said.

Mike smiled. "Sure there are!" he said. "I guess you don't know *everything* about Minnesota. This mall was built on the site of the Twins' first ballpark!"

Mike pointed to the giant wall behind the log flume ride. A red stadium chair was mounted to

the middle of the wall. "Metropolitan Stadium used to be here. It's where the Twins played when they first moved here from Washington, D.C.," Mike said. "Harmon Killebrew, one of their most famous players, hit a home run that went five hundred twenty-two feet and hit *that* chair. It was the longest home run ever in Metropolitan Stadium. That's why they put it up there."

"Neat!" Kate said.

"Come on," Mike said. "There's more!"

Kate followed Mike as he zigzagged past zip lines, a merry-go-round, and a climbing structure, until he was near the opposite corner.

"It's somewhere in front of one of these rides," Mike said as he scanned the floor.

"What is?" Kate asked.

"Metropolitan Stadium's home plate!" Mike

said. "There's a marker on the floor showing where the old home plate used to be. Help me look!"

Kate and Mike searched. A moment later, Kate spotted a brass marker shaped like a home plate in the concrete floor next to one of the rides. "I found it!" she called out.

She looked up to find Mike but was surprised to see two girls instead. Two identical twins! They both wore matching Twins jerseys and had black braids. The twin on the left had shiny gold charms on her braids, while the one on the right had baseball charms.

Just then, Mike came over. He looked at the brass plate in the floor and at the twins.

"Were you looking for Metropolitan's home plate?" the twin with the gold charms asked.

"Yes!" Kate said.

"We were, too!" the girls said at the same time.

"The Twins are our favorite team," the girl with the gold charms said. "We know everything about them. We're going to the game tonight, and our dad brought us here so we could see where Metropolitan Stadium used to be."

"We're going tonight, too," Mike said. "I'm Mike, and this is my cousin Kate."

"I'm Polly, and that's Molly," said the twin with the baseball charms. "Nice to meet you. Maybe we can hang out at the game tonight!"

Kate nodded. "That would be fun," she said. "But first, we're going on the roller coaster. Want to come?"

"Sure!" the twins said together.

"Let's go!" Kate said.

There were about twenty people waiting in line for the roller coaster. While they waited, Polly and Molly shared Minnesota Twins stories with Mike and Kate.

"We took a behind-the-scenes tour of the Twins' stadium last week," Polly said.

"We got to go into the Twins locker room," Molly said. "And down on the field. And they even showed us a hidden passage!"

"Wow, cool!" Mike said.

The roller-coaster line inched forward. It was almost their turn! As the group waited, Kate scanned the crowd of shoppers for her mother. Suddenly, she spotted someone.

"Hey, there's Pedro! Or is it Marco?" Kate wondered. She jumped up and down and waved her arms. "Pedro! Marco! Over here!" she called. "It's Mike and Kate!"

The twin baseball player towered over most of the other shoppers. He kept walking with his long, loping gait and looking around as if he didn't hear Kate. But a few of the shoppers near him glanced at Kate.

The roller-coaster line inched forward again as another car loaded. The line behind them had grown longer. "If the line wasn't so long, we could duck out and go talk to him!" Kate said.

"I got this," Mike said. He tucked a couple

of fingers in his mouth and gave a loud whistle. "Marco! Pedro!" he called out. "Over here!"

Mike's whistle got the twin's attention. He turned and looked at the kids.

Kate waved back. "Marco or Pedro!" she called. "It's Mike and Kate. We met yesterday at the game!"

The twin's eyes narrowed, and he frowned.

"Whoa!" Mike said. "What's the deal? He looks angry!"

"Maybe he doesn't like to be spotted when he's shopping," Kate said.

"Or maybe he's sleepwalking!" Molly said.

The baseball player suddenly turned away and disappeared into the crowd of shoppers.

"Why is Pedro or Marco acting so weird?" Kate asked.

"I don't know," Mike said. "But it's up to us to find out! We can put our detective skills to use at the Twins' stadium to figure out what's going on. If something's wrong with Marco or Pedro, the Twins might lose their games and not make the playoffs!"

"Next!" called the ride attendant. "Hey, you four, it's your turn!"

The kids stepped into the roller-coaster car.

"We'll look into the case of the strange twin at the game tonight," Mike said. "But right now, let's ride!"

Who's Lying?

"There they are!" Kate said. "Minnie and Paul!"

Kate pointed to a giant neon sign above center field. The sign was shaped like the state of Minnesota, with a big Minnesota Twins baseball logo at the top. Below were the twin baseball players, Minnie and Paul, shaking hands over the Mississippi River.

It was late afternoon, and Kate's mom had just brought Mike and Kate to the Twins' ballpark for that night's game. She was up in the pressroom, and Mike and Kate were on the flagpole terrace overlooking right field.

"We'll have to watch that because it lights up during the game," Kate said. "When the Twins hit a homer, Minnie and Paul shake hands. If the pitcher gets a strikeout, the corners flash. And if the Twins score a run, a light zips around the outside edge like a runner going around the bases!"

"Cool!" Mike said. They walked over to the flagpoles.

"Polly and Molly should be here soon. They said they'd meet us near the largest flagpole," Kate said. She gave it a rap with her knuckles. "It came from the Twins' original Metropolitan Stadium, where the mall is."

Mike and Kate waited. It was about an hour until game time. The Twins had finished their batting practice, and the Brewers were just starting theirs. Mike and Kate were waiting to meet the twin Twins. Kate had asked her mom to set up a meeting so they could try to figure out what was wrong with the twin they had spotted at the mall.

Some fans had come early to watch batting practice and to eat. Mike watched hungrily as people walked by with warm mini donuts caked with cinnamon sugar.

Mike gave a sniff and patted his stomach. "Mmm . . . I've got to try those," he said. "Some food might help me figure out what's wrong with the strange twin we saw earlier!"

"I'm saving room for some of the Minnesota State Fair food they have here," Kate said. "I read about it in the program. Like pork chops on a stick, corn dogs, deep-fried pickles, and cheese curds!"

"Yum!" Mike said.

Kate's phone buzzed with a message. As she glanced at it, someone called their names.

"Mike! Kate!" called two voices.

It was Polly and Molly, the twins from the mall.

"Good timing! We're on our way to meet Pedro and Marco. My mom just texted to tell us where they are!" Kate said. "Mike and I are going to try to figure out which twin was at the mall and what was wrong!"

"Cool!" Molly and Polly said.

The four made their way through the stadium to the team store. Just down the hall was a stairway marked SERVICE. After waiting a few minutes, the stairway door opened, and Pedro and Marco stepped out.

"Hey! What an impressive starting lineup!" Pedro said when he saw the four kids.

"These are our friends, Polly and Molly," Kate said.

Marco and Pedro looked at Polly and Molly and then at each other. "Are you seeing double?" Marco asked Pedro.

"Nope," Pedro said as he glanced at Marco and himself. "I'm actually seeing double-double!"

Marco and Pedro broke out laughing.

"Nice to meet you," Marco and Pedro said as they gave Polly and Molly fist bumps. "And it's good to see our friends Mike and Kate again!"

"Why didn't you say hello to us earlier today at the mall?" Kate asked.

Marco and Pedro looked at each other. "We weren't at the mall," Marco said.

"We saw you!" Mike said. "We weren't sure which one of you it was, but we called out to you, and you looked right at us!"

Marco scratched his head. "I guess we have a look-alike," he said. "We weren't at the mall today. I was home working on my yard, and Pedro was at the dentist." Marco turned to his brother. "Unless you were *lying* to me and had actually gone to the mall to buy me a birthday gift. My birthday is next week."

Pedro shook his head. "Nope. I didn't get you a gift, because I can never remember when your birthday is!" He held up his hands and shrugged.

Marco stared at him for a moment and then burst out laughing. He held up his right hand, and Pedro high-fived him.

SMACK!

"Nice one, bro," Marco said.

"Okay, so I *do* remember your birthday," Pedro said. "But only because it's the same day as mine!" He looked at Marco and smiled a toothy grin. "Maybe I'll get you a gift *next* year!"

Mike, Kate, Polly, and Molly all laughed.

Marco elbowed his brother. "We've got to go," he said. He tipped his hat to the kids. "Enjoy the game! And you should come to batting practice tomorrow! If we win tonight, tomorrow will be a super-big game. If we win that one, we'll make the playoffs! We'll leave your names with the security guard so you can come down to the field to watch!"

"Woo-hoo!" Mike shouted. "That will be a blast!"

"Thanks!" Polly and Molly said.

Marco smiled. "Let's go, Pedro."

Pedro waved to the group and then followed his brother back to the dugout.

"Wow, that was great!" Molly said.

"It sure was," Kate said. "I can't wait to watch batting practice tomorrow!"

Mike nodded. "That will be really cool," he said. "But you know what's not cool?"

"What?" Kate said.

"One of them was lying to us!" Mike said. "We *know* that one of them was at the mall today!"

"You're right," Kate said. "But why would he lie?"

"Because he is hiding something!" Mike said.

"What is he hiding?" Kate asked.

"I'm not sure," Mike said. "But I know how we can find out!"

A Second Spotting

"We'll investigate!" Mike said. "We've only talked to them together. But tomorrow we'll talk with them separately at batting practice. We'll try to get one of them to confess why he's lying about being at the mall!"

Kate nodded. "Good idea," she said.

Mike patted his belly. "All this detective work has made me hungry!"

"*¡Yo también tengo hambre!*" Kate said. She was teaching herself Spanish and liked to practice it whenever she could. "I'm hungry, too!"

"How about some of our great Minnesota food?" Polly asked.

"Oh yeah! Pork chop on a stick, here I come!" Mike said.

"Let's go!" Molly said.

The four raced to the nearest food stand. A little while later, they slipped into the seats near first base that Kate's mom had arranged, and started eating. Mike was taking big bites from a pork chop on a stick. Kate was nibbling on deep-fried pickles and chicken wings. And Polly and Molly were popping fried cheese curds into their mouths as the Brewers finished batting practice. Since it was getting closer to game time, fans were filling up the seats all around them.

"Have you seen the sculpture outside the

main gate?" Polly asked. "It's a huge golden glove that you can sit in!"

"Wow! That sounds great," Mike said. "I always knew I was a catch, but now I can take a picture and prove it!"

A little while later, the stadium's organ sprang to life with the notes of "Take Me Out to the Ball Game" floating through the ballpark. T.C. Bear marched around the infield to the music. When the music stopped, the announcer introduced the players. T.C. gave high-fives to the players as they ran out to take their places.

"Look! There's Pedro on first base and Marco on second base!" Polly said.

Everyone stood up for the national anthem, and then the game started with a bang. The first Milwaukee Brewers batter hit a line drive for a single! The center fielder threw the ball to Pedro on first base, but it was too late for an out.

The Twins fans rallied as their pitcher struck out the next Brewers batter. Shortly after, the Twins dispatched two more Milwaukee Brewers players, and the top of the first inning was over.

"Let's go, Twins!" Polly and Molly shouted together. They clapped as the first Twins batter stepped up to the plate.

The batter struck out after three pitches.

The second Twins batter hit a double, and the crowd went wild. They cheered as he slid into second.

Marco was up next. He strode to the plate and tapped it with his bat a few times, then took some practice swings. The Milwaukee Brewers pitcher threw the ball. Marco swung down and hard.

CRACK!

The ball sailed up into the darkening sky. Marco ran for first as the other runner headed around the bases. The ball flew high over the right-field seats. A home run! The Twins were ahead, 2–0.

Molly pointed to the giant Twins logo in center field. "Look!" she said.

The neon lights on the sign showed the

two baseball players shaking hands and the Mississippi River flowing.

"Cool!" Mike said.

The crowd cheered loudly for the next Twins batter. But, unfortunately, he hit a high pop fly for an out. The next batter struck out, and the inning was over. But the Twins were ahead!

The next few innings went by quickly. The Milwaukee Brewers scored once, reducing the Twins' lead to one. After the fourth inning, Mike, Kate, Molly, and Polly took a break for chocolate malt ice cream cups.

In the top of the fifth inning, the Milwaukee Brewers got runners on first and second base with no outs. It looked like they might have a chance to get ahead.

The next Brewers player hit a grounder to third base. The shortstop scooped up the ball with his bare hand, tagged the runner, and then threw the ball to Marco at second base. Marco tagged second base and rifled the ball to Pedro at first. It popped into Pedro's glove just before the Brewers runner crossed first base.

Out. Out. Out. The top of the inning was over!

"Wow! A TRIPLE PLAY!" Mike shouted. "I've never seen a triple play in person!"

"That's why we call them the Triple Play Twins!" Polly said. "They're really good at it. They've already made more triple plays this season than all the other teams combined!"

Kate stood up and clapped. "Let's go, Twins!" she called.

Neither team scored in the next few innings. The Twins were ahead as the ninth inning started. Three more outs and they'd win.

Mike nudged Kate. "Back in a few minutes," he said as he stood up to leave. "I'm going to the bathroom before the game ends."

Kate, Polly, and Molly watched the Twins strike out the last Milwaukee Brewers batter. Just as the Twins won the game, Mike bounded down the stairs and skidded to a stop.

"I saw him!" Mike yelled over the cheers of the crowd.

"Who?" Kate asked.

"The guy we saw yesterday! The one who probably threw the water balloon at the twins!" Mike said. "Quick, follow me!"

Fans had started to leave, and the walkways

were packed. But the kids expertly threaded their way through the crowd. Suddenly, Mike stopped and pointed to an ice cream stand near the bathrooms. "He was working there," he said. "Behind the counter!"

They hurried to the ice cream stand. But it was closed.

Mike spun around and scanned the crowd.

"He's gone!" Mike said.

"But I'll bet he'll be back tomorrow night," Kate said. "We can nab him then!"

A Third Possibility

"Is that him?" Polly asked.

Mike shook his head. "No," he said. "He had long blond hair and a black mustache. I don't see him."

It was the next night and Mike, Kate, Polly, and Molly were hiding behind a condiment stand on the main walkway of the Twins' ballpark. They were looking for the man who they suspected had thrown the water balloon at the twin Twins.

The gates to the stadium had just opened, and fans were starting to enter for batting practice.

"We need to get to batting practice," Kate said, "so we can question Pedro and Marco separately."

Mike and Kate had spent the afternoon exploring some of the lakes around Minneapolis with Kate's mom. They had walked across a long stone bridge over the Mississippi River downtown and gone to a flour mill museum nearby. Just before dinner, the group headed to the Twins' ballpark for batting practice. Mrs. Hopkins went to the pressroom to work while Mike and Kate met Molly and Polly at the front gate. If the Twins won tonight, they'd clinch a playoff spot for the first time in many years.

Mike scanned the food stand again but didn't see the suspect. "Okay," he said. "Let's come back after batting practice."

The four ran through the stadium and down an aisle leading to the field. When a security guard stopped them at the bottom, Mike explained Pedro and Marco's invitation to watch batting practice. The guard said something into a handheld radio and listened to the response. A moment later, he swung open the gate to the field and waved the kids on. "You can stand on the warning track behind the batting cage," he said. "But stay off the infield grass."

Mike, Kate, Polly, and Molly followed the warning track over to home plate. A few Twins players stood around the cage, talking or watching the other players bat.

A coach threw easy pitches from behind a protective screen on the mound. Batters hit one ball after another. Some balls sailed high into the air while others bounced along the freshly cut grass. Outfielders shagged the balls. They threw them back to the coach or tossed them to fans in the stands.

"There they are, waiting to bat!" Kate said.

"Marco! Pedro!" Mike called.

Pedro, with a number 12 on his back, turned around. He smiled and waved when he spotted the kids. He tapped his brother's shoulder and pointed. Marco turned and waved.

"I'll say hello after my turn!" Pedro called.

When Pedro got up a few minutes later, he hit four long fly balls in a row. One was caught by an outfielder, and three sailed over the right-field wall for home runs. Mike, Kate, Polly, and Molly cheered loudly. Pedro took some more swings, hitting a combination of grounders, a line drive, and a pop-up. When his turn was over, he walked over to the group.

"How'd I do?" he asked.

"Great!" Molly said.

"That was good!" Polly said. "Maybe you can hit one of those home runs in the game!"

"Let's hope!" Pedro replied. He took off his baseball cap and wiped his forehead.

"Pedro," Mike said. "Thanks for inviting us

to batting practice today. This is a blast. Just like your hit!"

Pedro laughed. "Glad you could make it," he said.

"So are we," Kate said. She looked for Marco. He was still in line for batting practice. "Hey, are you sure you or Marco weren't at the mall yesterday? We're certain we saw one of you."

Instead of answering, Pedro opened his mouth and said, "Ahhh . . ." He pointed to a tooth in the back of his mouth. "I wish I was at the mall!" he said. "But I was having a tooth filled. You can ask my dentist if you want!"

"Ouch!" Polly said.

Pedro smiled. "It's fine," he said. "I don't know what Marco was doing yesterday. I can tell you he wasn't at the dentist. Maybe he really did go to the mall to get me a birthday gift!"

Pedro glanced at the dugout. "Well, I've got to get ready for the game," he said. "See you later!"

He waved goodbye and disappeared into the tunnel that led to the locker room.

Mike scuffed at the warning track with his sneaker. "Sounds like Pedro is telling the truth," he said.

"If he is, that means we saw Marco," Polly said. "I wonder why he didn't admit it!"

"Let's find out," said Kate as she pointed to the batting cage. Marco had just stepped up to the plate for his turn. "We'll ask him again when he finishes hitting."

Marco missed the first three pitches that came at him. However, he finally connected on the fourth pitch with a powerhouse swing. A loud *CRACK!* split the air. The ball blasted high over center field.

But then it dropped right into the center fielder's glove!

Marco made contact on each of the next six pitches, but the hits were dribbling grounders that barely rolled past the pitcher.

Kate nudged Mike. "Not a great warm-up," she said.

Mike shook his head. "It was *really* bad!" he said. "If he doesn't hit better than that during the game, the Twins might not make the playoffs!"

"Marco! What's up?" the Twins manager called out. He had been watching from the dugout. "We need you to do better than that in the game tonight!"

Marco nodded and tipped his hat at the coach. He stood at the plate for a moment and gave it one last look. Then he walked away.

"Here he comes!" Mike whispered.

Marco approached the kids. But then he kept right on walking!

"Hey, Marco!" Kate called out.

But Marco didn't even look at the kids. Instead, he headed for the dugout.

"I'll get him," Polly said. She ran over to

Marco and tugged on his jersey. When he stopped, Polly said something to him and pointed at the group. Marco glanced at them, gave a sigh, and walked back with Polly.

"What do you kids want?" Marco asked.

Mike and Kate looked at each other. "Um," Mike said. "That was a good try up at the plate."

Marco shook his head. "Not really," he said. "Well, I gotta go."

"Wait!" Kate cried. "We know you were at the mall yesterday. And we know why you didn't admit it!"

Marco's eyebrows raised up and his jaw tightened. "Wh-what do you mean?" he asked.

Kate leaned closer to him and studied his face for a moment. "We know that Pedro was at the dentist, so that means it was you we saw at the mall, Marco. We think you were buying

Pedro a birthday gift and didn't want to admit it in front of him!"

"Um, yeah, you're right," he said. "That's it! I was buying a gift and didn't want him to know. So I couldn't tell you when we talked."

He glanced one more time at the batters hitting practice balls. "Listen, I have to go," he said. "I forgot my bat over there."

"That was weird," Molly said after Marco left.

Mike nodded. "He seemed distracted or something," he said.

"What's even weirder," Kate said, "is that I don't know who that was!"

"What do you mean?" Mike asked. "There's Pedro and Marco. That was Marco."

"No, it wasn't!" Kate said. "Did you see me lean in when I was talking to him?"

Polly, Molly, and Mike nodded.

"I was checking out his face," Kate said. "Something wasn't right!"

"What do you mean?" Mike asked.

Kate pointed to the twin. He was picking up his bat near the batting cage.

"He's an imposter!" she said.

A Second Surprise!

"I don't know who he is," Kate said. "But he's not Marco or Pedro! And I can prove it."

"How do you know?" Molly asked.

Kate glanced at the twin. He had picked up his baseball bat and was talking to another player.

"The scar!" Kate said. "Remember when Marco showed us his scar and Pedro showed us the chip on his tooth?"

Mike nodded.

"Well, this guy doesn't have either a scar or a chip on his tooth!" Kate said. "He's an imposter!"

"Wow!" Polly and Molly said at the same time.

"Whoever he is, his name isn't Marco," Kate said. "That's why he didn't turn around when we called him before batting practice. And it's why he didn't stop when we called out Marco's name as he walked by!"

All four glanced over at the imposter. He was still talking to one of the Twins players.

"We've got to figure out what to do before the game starts," Kate said. "If he hits like that in the game, the Twins may lose!"

"And if he's really not Marco, the Twins could be disqualified for breaking the rules!" Mike said. "If we don't stop the imposter, the Twins will be in trouble!"

"That would be terrible!" Molly said. "Twins fans have been waiting a long time to make the playoffs again!"

"And what about the *real* Marco?" Polly asked. "What if he's been kidnapped or something? We need to find him before the game starts!"

The imposter finished talking to the Twins player. He had slung the bat over his shoulder and was walking to the dugout.

"I've got an idea," Mike said. He pulled a baseball out of his pocket. It was the one that Marco and Pedro had signed for him yesterday. Mike gave a sharp whistle. When the imposter glanced over to see who had whistled, Mike tossed the baseball to him. "Heads up!" he called.

The imposter stopped in his tracks and caught the ball.

Mike motioned for the others to follow him.

They all ran over to the imposter and surrounded him.

The imposter held out the ball. "Thanks, but I don't have time to play catch," he said.

Mike held out his marker. "We just wanted you to sign it," he said.

The imposter shrugged and quickly scribbled a signature on the ball. He handed it back to Mike and took a step forward to leave. Mike quickly studied the ball and then held it up.

"This isn't your signature," Mike said.

"What do you mean?" the man said. "I just signed it in front of you."

Mike spun the ball around to the other side so that Pedro's and Marco's signatures showed. "We got the real Marco's signature already," he said. He flipped the ball back. "But your signature is completely different!"

The imposter shrugged. "So what?" he said.

"Sometimes I change my signature. What's that mean?"

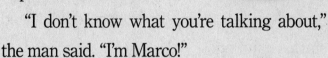

"It means you're an imposter!" Kate said.

"I don't know what you're talking about," the man said. "I'm Marco!"

"No, you're not," Mike said. "Marco and Pedro showed us how to tell them apart by the scar on Marco's chin."

"You're wrong!" the man said.

"No, we're not," Kate said. "You don't have a scar! We don't know who you are, but you're not Pedro's brother Marco."

"And you definitely don't play for the Minnesota Twins!" Mike said.

Mike nodded to Polly and Molly. "Can you please bring the security guard over from the gate?"

"Sure!" Polly and Molly said. They took off.

Suddenly, the imposter pulled the bat off his shoulder and held it in front of him like a snowplow. Then he used it to push Mike and Kate out of the way, knocking them over. Once he had passed them, he dropped the bat and started running!

"Stop him!" Kate called out as she stood up. "Polly! Molly!"

"Go!" Mike said. He and Kate chased after him.

The man bounded across the field and jumped the infield wall. His long legs carried him fast. He tore up the aisle to the main walkway as Mike, Kate, Polly, and Molly scrambled to keep up. Tracking the man wasn't easy since fans had started to stream in for the game. The kids had to weave between them as they ran.

At the top of the stairs, the man leapt to the

left, through a school group clustered on the walkway. When Mike, Kate, Polly, and Molly reached the top, they ran around the group and looked for any sign of the imposter.

But he was gone!

Out of Storage

Polly, Molly, Mike, and Kate spun around to see if they could spot the imposter. But there was no trace of him. All they saw were fans buying food, looking for restrooms, or walking to their seats. And lots of places to escape. Stairways to the upper levels, elevators that went up and down, and an exit in the corner that led outside. But there was no sign of the fake Marco.

"Now what?" Molly asked. "He could be anywhere!"

"The first thing he'll probably try to do is change out of that uniform," Kate said. "It's too easy to spot. Then he'll probably try to leave the ballpark."

"And what about the real Marco?" Polly asked. "We need to find him before the game starts."

"We don't have much time," Kate said. "First pitch is in forty-five minutes! We have to track down the real Marco before the manager submits the lineup card to the umpire!"

"Let's split up!" Mike said. "Polly and Molly, you keep looking for fake Marco. See if he's hiding anywhere. And ask the ushers and security guards if they've seen him."

"Okay!" Polly and Molly answered.

"Kate and I will go tell Pedro what's happened and see if he can help us," Mike said. "He'll have to tell his manager, too."

Mike and Kate gave Polly and Molly fist bumps, and then both groups headed off. Polly and Molly started down the main hallway, checking all the doors. Mike and Kate ran through the stadium and down to the field. They went to the same security guard who had let them on the field for batting practice. He nodded at them as they approached.

"Can you please contact Pedro?" Kate said. "Tell him that Mike and Kate have something very important to tell him."

The security guard pulled out his handheld radio and relayed the message. A moment later, his radio squawked.

"Pedro says he'll be here in a minute," the guard said. "Stay put."

A moment later, Pedro sprinted over from the dugout.

"What's up?" Pedro asked. "You haven't

seen Marco, have you? He never came back to the locker room after batting practice!"

"No, we haven't," Mike said. "But we saw a fake Marco!"

Pedro's eyes opened wide. "What do you mean a fake Marco?" he asked.

"We think someone is impersonating Marco for some reason," Mike said. Then he and Kate quickly brought Pedro up to date on what they'd discovered.

"Wow! That's unbelievable!" Pedro said. "Good job stopping the fake Marco from play-ing, but now we have to find the real one!"

"Maybe he locked the real Marco up at home?"

Pedro shook his head. "Nope, I picked him up this morning, and it was the real Marco," he said. "I know it was him because the scar on his chin stood out. It was covered in white sugar from a powdered donut he had just eaten. But we split up when we got to the ballpark. He wanted to work out, but I needed to ice my arm. It must have happened here, after that."

Pedro rooted around in his back pants pocket and pulled out a piece of paper. "This must have something to do with it, though," he said. "I found this note near Marco's locker just now."

Pedro unfolded the piece of paper. The note read:

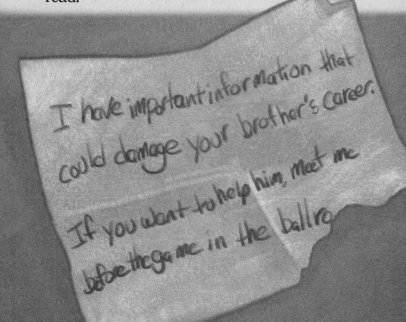

I have important information that could damage your brother's career. If you want to help him, meet me before the game in the ballr[o]

"The ballro?" Kate asked. "What's a ballro?"

"I don't know!" Pedro said. He pointed to the bottom edge of the paper. It was torn. "That's the problem. It's ripped right at the end. I had no idea where to look!"

"We need to find that room right away!" Mike said.

"But there are hundreds of rooms here," Pedro said. "How are we going to do it?"

"We have Polly and Molly working on that," Mike said. "Follow me!"

"Okay," Pedro said. "Lead the way!"

Pedro hopped over the infield wall and bounded up the steps after Mike and Kate. They ran through the stadium to the area where they had left Polly and Molly.

"There's Polly!" Kate said. "Did you find anything?"

Polly and Molly held up their hands and

shook their heads. "Nothing," Polly said. "No sign of the fake Marco or the real one!"

Kate held out the note. "We have a new clue," she said. "Pedro found this. But we don't know what a ballro is!"

Molly and Polly read the note. A smile crept across their faces.

"We do!" Molly said.

"You do?" Mike asked. "What is it?"

"It's the ball room!" Polly said. "Where they store the baseballs. It just looked like *ballro* on the note because of the torn part and the sloppy handwriting! If you look closely, it says 'ball ro' not 'ballro.'"

"But that's on the other side of the stadium!" Pedro said. "We don't have time to get there before the game starts."

"Actually, we know a shortcut," Polly said.

"We learned about it on our tour last week. Follow us!"

Molly and Polly raced down the walkway to a service entrance near the exit. Polly pushed through it and bounded down a set of stairs. At the bottom was a long service hallway. The group followed as Polly and Molly ran the length of the hallway. They stopped at the end.

In front of them was a door marked BALL ROOM. Nearby were doors marked SPRINKLER PARTS ROOM and CLEANING SUPPLIES ROOM.

Kate stepped up to the door and turned the handle. It rotated, but the door didn't open. A big combination lock held the door shut.

Kate banged on the door. "Anyone in there?" she called, and then put her ear against the door. Her eyes grew wide. "I think I heard someone!" she said.

Mike and Pedro put their ears against the door and listened. Muffled sounds came from the other side.

"Someone's in there!" Mike said.

"Move away, kids," Pedro said. They shifted to the side while Pedro took a few steps back. He ran straight for the door to the ball room and plowed into it with his right shoulder. The door shook for a moment but remained shut. Pedro stepped away from the door, rubbing his shoulder.

"It's no use," he said. "That's a metal door with a metal door frame. That lock is too sturdy. We won't get in unless we find someone who knows the combination. I can call the equipment manager, but he's usually hard to track down."

Mike studied the sign on the door. "Baseball storage," he said. He stepped forward. "Or unless someone can guess the combination!"

Mike grabbed the lock and spun the dial. "Teams go through about ninety baseballs in a game," he said. "So I'm trying the numbers 0-9-0!"

He spun the lock dial back and forth. When he hit the second zero, he gave the lock a tug.

It didn't move at all.

"Rats!" Kate said. "Nice try."

"Wait, I've got another idea," Mike said. He spun the dial to stop on the numbers 1-0-8.

"Why one hundred and eight?" Polly asked.

"One hundred and eight stitches!" Mike said. "That's how many double stitches of red cotton thread there are on a baseball!"

Mike gave the lock a sharp tug. It unlocked! He pulled it up and turned the door handle. The door swung wide open!

"Wow! Great job, Mike!" Kate said.

Mike, Kate, Molly, Polly, and Pedro ran through the open door.

Tied to a chair in the middle of the storage room was Marco!

He had a piece of cloth over his mouth so he couldn't yell. Pedro carefully pulled off the cloth while Mike untied Marco.

"I'm so happy to see you!" Marco said. "How'd you find me?"

Pedro took out the note he had found near

Marco's locker. "I found this on the floor!" he said.

A big smile crossed Marco's face. "I'm really glad you did," he said. He stood up and stretched. "I was worried about that note so I came here to find out what I could do. But as soon as I entered the room, someone slipped a bag over my head and tied me up. He took the bag off when he left, but I didn't see him. I could have been here a long time."

"I think that's what the fake Marco was counting on," Mike said.

Marco stared at Mike. "Fake Marco?" he asked.

"Yes," Mike answered. "A guy who looks almost exactly like you and Pedro is the one who locked you in this room. He was pretending to be you at batting practice, but Kate noticed he wasn't you when we talked to him. We confronted him, but he ran away and disappeared. That's when we looked for you."

"How did you know that the guy you were talking to wasn't really me?" Marco asked.

"It was easy," Kate said. "He didn't have a scar! But he looked exactly like both of you."

The brothers glanced at each other. Then they both let out a big sigh.

Marco nodded and motioned to Pedro and himself. "We have a confession to make," he said. "We're not actually twins."

"What do you mean?" Mike asked. "You're brothers born at the same time. You look exactly alike. You must be twins!"

A big smile spread across Kate's face. "Now I get it!" she said. "Marco's right, Mike. They're not twins. They're triplets!"

A Triple Play

"Triplets?" Mike asked.

Marco and Pedro nodded.

"The fake Marco is actually our brother Leo," Pedro said. "As Kate said, Marco, Leo, and I are triplets, not twins."

"But why would your own brother lock you in a room and impersonate you?" Polly asked. "That seems really mean."

"Leo always felt left out of our family," Pedro said. "Growing up, he really wanted to be a great baseball player, but he never bothered to practice. And when we made it to the Twins and he didn't, he got really jealous."

Marco nodded. "We felt bad for him and tried to find ways to keep him connected to baseball," he said. "But Leo couldn't stand that we were playing baseball and he wasn't. He disappeared. We haven't seen him in a couple of years."

"I guess he's back," Pedro said.

"He's back, and he wants to play baseball," Kate said.

"Wow! Play baseball!" Pedro said. He checked his watch. "The game is going to start soon. We need to get down to the field, or they'll take us out of the lineup!" He turned to Marco. "Are you okay to play?"

Marco clenched his hands around an imaginary baseball bat and took a swing. "It takes more than a jealous brother to stop me!" he said.

"Let's go!" Pedro said. He headed for the door. "We have to focus on this game. We can figure out what to do about Leo later. For now, don't follow the directions on any more notes you find in your locker!"

Marco smiled and gave his brother a high five. "You've got it!" he said. He nodded to Polly, Molly, Mike, and Kate. "Thanks so much for rescuing me! All four of you are all-stars in my book!"

The brothers waved goodbye. "See you later!" they said as they left.

Mike headed for the door. "We should get to our seats," he said. "Last one there has to buy deep-fried pickles for everyone!"

Kate, Polly, and Molly scrambled though the stadium after Mike.

During the race to their seats, Mike got distracted when he passed a hot donut machine. He skidded to a stop to watch it pump out miniature cinnamon sugar donuts. By the time he remembered the race, the others were already in their seats.

"Okay, okay," Mike said as he slipped into the last seat in the row. "I guess I lost that race. But I might have won the snack food competition!" He held out a white bag filled with tiny, hot cinnamon sugar donuts.

Polly, Molly, and Kate all grabbed a few and started munching.

"Yum!" Molly said.

"These are great!" Polly said.

Mike wiped some cinnamon sugar from his lip. "Let's hope the Twins are just as good today as these donuts!" he said.

During the early innings, the Twins were in charge. Their pitcher struck out one batter after another. And their hitters kept getting on base and scoring runs. By the fourth inning, the Twins were ahead by three!

But things fell apart in the fifth inning. A Brewers batter hit a huge solo home run. And the next two batters both hit singles.

"Oh no!" Mike said. "With no outs and two men on base, the Brewers could tie up the score! Let's go, Twins!"

The first couple of pitches looked good for the Twins. The Twins pitcher got ahead in the count, two balls, no strikes. But on the third pitch, the Brewers batter swung. He connected for a rolling grounder down the third-base line.

The third baseman scooped up the ball and tagged the base. Then he threw it to Marco at second base. Marco stepped on the bag and rifled it to Pedro at first. The ball snapped into his glove just before the batter tagged the base.

"ANOTHER TRIPLE PLAY!" Kate screamed.

"Woo-hoo!" Mike yelled.

The Twins fans exploded with cheers and claps.

"That saved the game!" Polly said.

Polly, Molly, Mike, and Kate gave each other high fives as the Twins ran off the field.

"Seems like a good time to get a PowerPunch," Mike said. "I'll be back soon." He bounded up the stairs.

Mike returned a few minutes later.

"Come with me," he said. "I think I found something important."

Mike sprang up the stairs and ran for one of the food counters. Kate, Polly, and Molly quickly followed.

Mike stopped in the main hallway, across from the ice cream stand. He pointed to a tall man working the cash register. "I think I found our man," he said.

"You're right!" Kate said. "That looks exactly like the guy we chased at the Saints' ballpark."

Mike nodded. "Yup," he said. "I think that's

the guy who threw the water balloon. And maybe the guy who locked Marco in the ball room!"

"What do you mean?" Polly asked. "That doesn't look like Leo! Leo looks exactly like Marco. That guy's got blond hair and a mustache!"

Mike waved his hand. "Follow me," he said. "I'll show you what I found out when I bought my drink." Mike strode over to the ice cream stand. Kate, Polly, and Molly followed. Mike waited for the woman ahead of him to finish. When she did, Mike stepped up to the counter.

"Can I help you?" the tall man asked.

Mike turned to the other three. "Look closely at him!" he whispered. Mike turned back to the man. "Ummm, I'm trying to decide between the chocolate and the vanilla," he said.

While the man was waiting for Mike to decide, Kate, Polly, and Molly leaned forward to study him.

Kate nudged Mike and gave him a thumbs-up. He nodded back.

"Hurry up, kids!" the worker said. "We have other people waiting."

Mike leaned over the counter, close to the worker. "Yes, you can help me," he said. In a flash, he reached up and grabbed ahold of the man's mustache.

"Ouch!" The man raised his hand. But it was too late!

Mike ripped the fake mustache off his upper lip! As the man fumbled to cover his face, Mike tugged on his long blond hair. A wig came flying off his head! Underneath, he had the same buzz cut that Pedro and Marco had. He looked exactly like them!

"And you can help your brothers, too, Leo," Mike said. "By apologizing to them!"

10

Triple Play Triplets

"Why do you think Marco and Pedro want to meet with us?" Polly asked.

"I don't know," Kate said. "But we're about to find out!"

It was the next day. Mike, Kate, and Mrs. Hopkins had just joined Polly and Molly near the front gate of the stadium for an afternoon game. Marco and Pedro had asked to see all of them after batting practice.

After Mike yanked off Leo's disguise at the

ice cream stand, Leo had agreed to find his brothers when the game was done and apologize. "I didn't want to hurt anyone," he had said. "I just wanted a chance to play in a real game." Marco and Pedro accepted Leo's apology and asked him to come back after the next day's game.

When Mike, Kate, Mrs. Hopkins, Polly, and Molly reached the side of the Twins dugout, a security guard spotted them and waved them through the gate onto the field. He pointed to the on-deck circle, where Pedro, Marco, and Leo stood.

"There you are," Marco said. He picked up a bag near his feet and opened it. "We have something for you."

"Cool!" Mike said.

"Close your eyes and hold out your hands," Pedro said.

Mike, Kate, Polly, and Molly did as they were told.

"I hope it's not a pile of cheese curds," Mike said.

Pedro and Marco laughed. "No, but it is something you'd find at the Twins' ballpark!" Marco said. He placed something in the kids' outstretched hands.

"It tickles!" Polly said.

"It's soft," Molly said. "Can we open our eyes?"

"Okay!" Marco and Pedro said.

The four kids opened their eyes. They were each holding a soft, furry stuffed animal. It was a plush version of the Twins' mascot, T.C. Bear! He was wearing a Twins baseball cap and jersey.

"I love T.C.!" Kate said. She gave the stuffed bear a hug. "This is great! Thank you."

"Thank you!" Polly and Molly said.

"You're welcome," Marco said. "But check out the back of the jersey."

The four kids turned their stuffed bears around. On the back was T.C.'s number, 00. But to the sides and top of the numbers were three signatures.

"Leo, Pedro, and I signed each of your bears so you'd remember us," Marco said.

"Don't worry, we'll never forget you," Kate said. "I'm glad we have Leo's autograph, too. I hope things work out."

"I think they will," Pedro said.

"Mom had a long talk with the three of us last night, right, Leo?" Marco said.

Leo scuffed the grass with his foot. "Um, yup," he said softly. "A *long* talk."

"And what did she tell you?" Marco asked.

"She told me to apologize for hurting my

brother and causing trouble," Leo said. He glanced up at Mike, Kate, Polly, and Molly. "I already apologized to Marco and Pedro. But I also need to apologize to you all. I'm sorry I lied to you and knocked you over after batting practice."

"Thanks," Mike and Kate said.

"And what else did Mom say?" Pedro asked.

"Families take care of each other," Leo said. He looked up at Marco and Pedro. "And stick together."

"That's right," Pedro said. "And Marco and I are going to do a better job of sticking together with Leo." He reached out and gave Leo's shoulder a shake.

"I'm afraid we can't convince the coach to put Leo on the team," Marco said. "But Leo's going to be spending a lot of time in the ball-park, helping us work out. It just so happens that he's an excellent personal trainer."

"And he's going to help manage our fan club and charity appearances," Pedro said. "The twin Twins have enough work for three people!"

Leo gave a big smile. He stretched out his arms and draped them over Marco's and Pedro's shoulders.

"Even though I don't deserve it after what I did, these two guys are giving me a second chance," Leo said. "I'm going to work hard to be a better brother. I'd rather hold on to my brothers than my jealousy. It's fun to be around them again. And even though I'm not good enough to make the team, I'll find other ways to contribute."

Pedro and Marco gave Leo a side hug and tousled his hair.

"Well, maybe if you listen to us, you'll be good enough to play third base next year," Marco said. "Then the three of us could be the Triple Play Triplets!"

Dugout Notes

☆ Minnesota Twins ☆

Old homes. When the Senators moved from Washington, D.C., to become the Minnesota Twins, they played in Metropolitan Stadium. Between 1961 and 1981, both the Twins and the Minnesota Vikings football team used the stadium. In 1982, the Twins moved to the Metrodome in downtown Minneapolis. The Metrodome had a white fiberglass roof that was held up by air pressure, like a balloon. The white color of the

99

roof made it hard for fielders to see fly balls. The Twins' original home, Metropolitan Stadium, was later torn down, and the Mall of America was built there.

Hammerin' Harmon. Hard-hitting Harmon Killebrew spent more than twenty years playing first base, third base, and left field for the Washington Senators and the Minnesota Twins. The Hall of Fame player was known for long and strong home runs. His 522-foot home run at Metropolitan Stadium set a record.

Local stones. The outside of the Twins' ballpark is built from tan-colored limestone from Minnesota. The local limestone is also featured inside the stadium behind home plate and in other locations.

A giant golden glove. Outside the entrance to the stadium is a giant golden glove that's big enough to sit in! Lots of Twins fans have their pictures taken as they're nestled inside the palm of the glove. The golden sculpture honors all the Twins players who have won Gold Glove Awards over the years. Pitcher Jim Kaat won sixteen in a row. Kirby Puckett won six, and Torii Hunter won seven with the Twins.

Hanging out. There's an unusual overhang in deep right field at the Twins' ballpark. A part of the seating area, known as the Overlook, extends over the right field warning track by eight and a half feet. That's enough to interfere with a ball that might be caught for an out by a speedy right fielder!

Skyway connectors. While Minneapolis summers can be beautiful, it does get cold and snowy in the city during the winter. That's why there's eleven miles of enclosed footbridges that cross over streets to link downtown buildings. The system covers more than eighty city blocks!

Lifesize heroes. Just outside the Twins' ballpark are large bronze action statues honoring famous Twins players. Fans can walk up to Kirby Puckett as he celebrates his walk-off home run, or touch Harmon Killebrew's bat as he swings it. Other statues include Tony Oliva, Rod Carew, and former Twins owners Calvin Griffith and Carl and Eloise Pohlad.

A moving sculpture. Located on a tall wall in the main plaza, the Wind Veil sculpture is composed of 51,000 small pieces of aluminum stitched together in a way that lets each piece flutter with the wind. Fans can watch as the wind blows patterns across the tiny moving panels.

World Series winners. The Washington Senators won the World Series in 1924. The Minnesota Twins won the World Series in 1987 and 1991. The 1991 series against the Atlanta Braves was especially exciting. It was voted one of the best ever. Going into game six, the Twins were behind by one

game and needed to win. An amazing catch by Kirby Puckett saved the day. Then a walk-off home run by Puckett in the eleventh inning won the game for the Twins. The Twins won game seven 1–0 the following night to win the series.

Legendary gates. The stadium gates aren't numbered the way they are at other ballparks. Instead, the Twins numbered the entrance gates in honor of important Twins players. For example, the center-field gate is 3 for Harmon Killebrew, while the right-field gate is 34 for Kirby Puckett, and home plate's gate is 14 for Kent Hrbek.

Catch the next baseball mystery in

BALLPARK Mysteries 18

Mike and Kate are in Atlanta to watch the Braves play the Boston Red Sox. But things change quickly when they discover a huge theft! The bat and ball that Hank Aaron used to hit his record-breaking 715th home run are missing. Can Mike and Kate find Hank Aaron's treasures before they're gone forever?

Coming in 2022!

Magical adventures are just a page-turn away!

For ballerina and fairy and vampire lovers

ISADORA MOON

For unicorn lovers

UNICORN ACADEMY

For dog lovers

PUPPY PIRATES

For mermaid and cat lovers

PuRRMaids

Isadora Moon: cover art © Harriet Muncaster. Unicorn Academy: cover art © Lucy Truman. Puppy Pirates: cover art © Luz Tapia. Purrmaids: cover art © Andrew Farley. Purrmaids™ is a registered trademark of KIKIDOODLE LLC and is used under license from KIKIDOODLE LLC.